THIS WALKER BOOK BELONGS TO:

_____

_____

_____

To Claire, with love

First published 2006 by Walker Books Ltd
87 Vauxhall Walk, London SE11 5HJ

This edition produced 2006 for Bookstart

10 9 8 7 6 5 4 3 2 1

© 2006 Petr Horáček

The right of Petr Horáček to be identified as author/illustrator
of this work has been asserted by him in accordance with
the Copyright, Designs and Patents Act 1988

This book has been typeset in Futura T Light

Printed in China

British Library Cataloguing in Publication Data: a catalogue record for
this book is available from the British Library

ISBN 978-1-4063-0722-1

www.walkerbooks.co.uk

WALKER BOOKS
AND SUBSIDIARIES
LONDON • BOSTON • SYDNEY • AUCKLAND

One day Suzy Goose
looked around. She was just like
everybody else. I wish I could
be different, she thought.

Silly Suzy Goose

Petr Horáček

If I was
a bat I could hang
upside down and

FLAP

my wings

If I was a penguin I could slip and

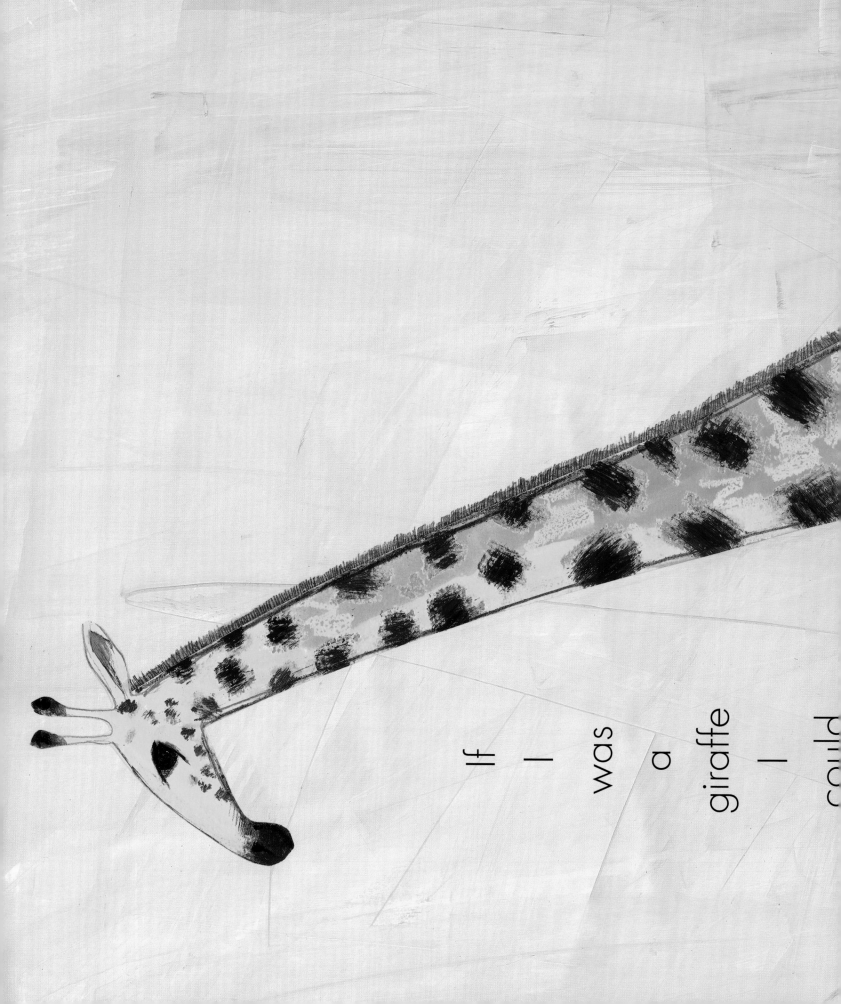

If
I
was
a
giraffe
I
could

STRETCH

up
high

If I was an elephant I could splish and

If I was a kangaroo I could jump, jump, jump and JUMP

If I was an ostrich I could
RUN really fast

If I
was a
seal
I could

SWIM

under
the water

If I was a lion I could roar

and **ROAR**

Rroarrhonk!

said Suzy Goose.

But the lion didn't notice.
So Suzy Goose
tried again.
How silly!

This time the lion did notice.

And he

didn't

like it

at all.

Suzy Goose
yelled
and
stretched

and swam

and
jumped

and
splashed

and slid

and flapped
and ran ...

all
the
way
back
to
the
others.

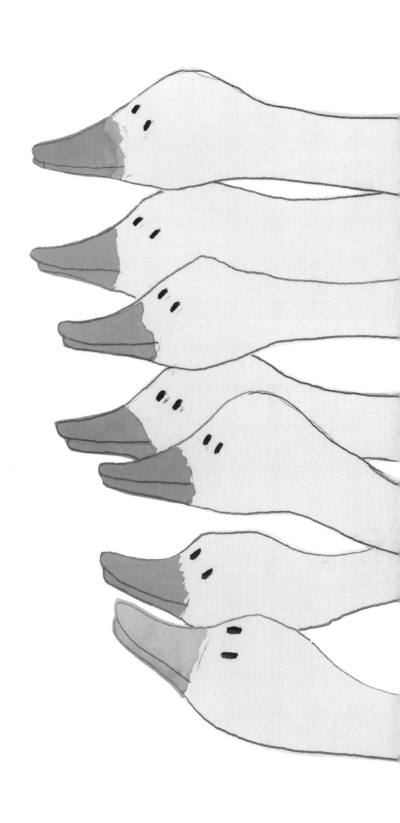

Just in time!

Perhaps it is better to be just like everyone else, thought Suzy Goose ...

but not
all the time.